VIVAR

# VIVARIUM

Poems by Maarja Pärtna

TRANSLATED BY JAYDE WILL

*The translation and publication of this book was made possible by a grant from the Traducta programme of the Cultural Endowment of Estonia.*

EESTI KULTUURKAPITAL

THE EMMA PRESS

First published in Estonia as *Vivaarium* by Elusamus in 2019.
First published in the UK in 2020 by The Emma Press Ltd.

Poems © Maarja Pärtna 2019
English-language translation © Jayde Will 2020
Cover image © Lilli-Krõõt Repnau 2019
Edited by Emma Dai'an Wright

ISBN 978-1-912915-42-2

A CIP catalogue record of this book
is available from the British Library.

Printed and bound in the UK
by Oxuniprint, Oxford.

The Emma Press
theemmapress.com
hello@theemmapress.com
Birmingham, UK

# CONTENTS

## house

I sometimes visit those places
that are no longer the same –
their smells, surfaces, light
and shadows

still haunt me there. I am standing
on a threshold that doesn't exist
in a house whose very foundations
have been carried back to the fields

stone by stone. I stand
in the middle of the field
my hands blistered

and I look over my shoulder
at the house through time
that's standing still.

in an empty room a door
begins to take shape around me
one that was impossible
for me to go through before.

most probably I never
really left this place.

## *threshold*

time made me a stranger
in this house where I used to belong.
I am framed by the doorway, I stand

here like in a photo that doesn't want
to be exposed. nothing is exactly
what it appears to be – the walls hide
hidden doors and the doors hidden walls.

the river I wanted to wade in
a second time has dried up
and no amount of self-knowledge
will bring it flowing back to that old riverbed.

## self-portrait

you moved a little bit
when I took your photo.
now two edges slice your body in half
from your right shoulder to your left breast.

you look right at me reproachfully
squint a little, your tense face showing
clear defiance at being silenced
and forced to stay put

in this photo where I
captured you and made you become
unchangeable, defined –

you look right at me in silence, frozen
but I know: you are already
looking for a way out

your lips slightly parted
the tip of your tongue forming
the beginning of this poem.

## *keyhole*

when at last I leave this photo
I have no voice nor a name
which is why you look at me

without recognising yourself
and that's precisely how, through
that silence like a keyhole, I am able
to get out. a piercing wind

blows from the side of the house
pushes me down the dry riverbed

but ahead the century grows ever narrower
taking everything that I knew
with it into the darkness beyond.

## *the well*

the shape I take
in an ever-warming future
does not depend on things at hand.
faced with a wall I fit

windows that open into windowless rooms
steps that finish at the beginning of steps –
everything in sight falls easily
into the onlooker's eye.

at the bottom of the eye is a well
down the well is a city
in the centre of that city

at the well's edge
I lean over and fall
into selflessness, saying

*the name you give me*
*will show first and foremost*
*who you really want to be.*

## garden

this photo of a starling singing
taken at home in my garden
that last Soviet summer

can show nothing
of his skill in copying
the voices around him.

his nest is attached
to the cherry tree –
I stand beneath in a puddle
in small blue rubber boots

begin to realise slowly
how hopeless it is to try and direct
the path of words in this world.

the starling from a crown of buds
imitates, among others,
a cat

the cat
sits on the top rung
of the ladder leading to the hayloft

her look gives nothing away
of what she thinks
of this imitation.

my look is giving nothing away
of what that kind of future
means to me.

## tourist visa

it was July when I returned to that old house
by the woods in the middle of a busy hay harvest –
this is why no one had noticed it.

all that was left
of the two green military barracks
were some piles of bricks

the outlines of rooms, corners and thresholds
still detectable in the grass
that had grown tall, still familiar

to my hands and feet. even the asphalt roads
had surrendered to the onslaught of grass
except for a few lonely patches.

the ceiling had collapsed, along with
that thing I couldn't find a name for back then
when I was five years old – but now?

now blackcurrants and gooseberries.
white translucent apple trees
growing through frameless windows

through non-existent walls
right into the kitchen and living room

beneath a piercingly blue sky.
it didn't seem like they remembered much
at all from their life as pruned garden plants.

## communal flat

they turned my building
upside down from cellar to attic
they turned it on its head from top to bottom
they broke down the door of my home and insisted

it was living space assigned
to them starting from now.

in rooms without an address
in a country world maps
don't remember anymore

the footprints of strangers' lives
on exhausted steps of staircases
the jangling of the cold latch
on the downstairs door

the faded colour of floorboards
the plywood chairs with worn-out seats
lined up against the wall

in extremely tiny rooms
in a country where an immense history
forced strangers to live in close quarters

until smoke from the stove began blowing in
the stove's tile wall collapsed
the paint peeled

and no one cared in the least
how I liked to sit there
in the mornings all by myself
in my home
in my kitchen

the smell of freshly-brewed coffee
a vase with a lilac branch

or its shadow
like a memory left without a body.

## *blackout / arrival*

close the curtains
to hide yourself. in the blackout
the city dissolves into the landscape
in the world's closing fist.

when the air raid comes
they might crush and destroy you
but this way it's harder to find you –
at least that's what you hope.

                when you
reached the opposite shore in a boat
the light left you speechless.
from that dark and ruined city
now to all these lights, the warmth
of domestic life shining through
the brightly-lit windows

everything you missed for so long –
the normality and ordinariness
left you at a loss for words.

seventy years later in this city on this street
in the same apartment you once left behind
someone pores over your letters
tries to understand this moment.

perhaps this person is me.

                what do I know
about darkness
and the light that follows it?

what would you say if you saw my struggle
to will myself beyond my peaceful surroundings
of switches, lamps and screens –
doorways into an endless space?

I imagine holding my breath
while I wait inside a tightly closed fist
where no pairs of car lights
part the darkness ahead

a place no ringing
of a phone can reach.

a place no lamp turns on
above the front door to light the way
for the one who arrives home so very late.

## shelter 1

they keep attacking
which is why he must build it
underground in the old cellar

fill it with water bottles and tins of food
bring blankets, matches and candles
shotgun cartridges, a shotgun.

at some point they will certainly arrive –
eyes wide open like the umbels of hogweed
sharp teeth bared like so many young minks.

contain them? is it even possible
to contain relentless thoughts that pierce the skull
like rusty swords that cut the earth
in spring when fields are ploughed

or birch roots that burrow ever deeper
through the centuries
through the strongest doors of faith.

# *mindscape*

this city turned inside-out
is a green mindscape, an architecture
of neural networks, desire paths and wanderings

in the bindweed between skyscrapers.
in a ravine beneath an ivy footbridge
lie machines, birds and human beings
completely intertwined.

in a narrow sidewalk crack
a cranesbill grows, between its blue blossoms
a replica of the world made of spider silk –

I close my palms around it
to keep its laws intact. a green woman
rides the underground at night

the land where she was born
will be swallowed up by water.

in this small role
I carry her heart in my breast.
my place is a border and all my shelters
are only temporary.

*shelter* II

all my shelters
are only temporary. something is always
left undone, unfinished, unsaid –
something always remains

the crests of night-time waves
hope, escape, the illegible scrawlings
of jackdaw flocks in the sky
above a scarred city.

I don't want to stand on
the narrow fault line of history
but I won't hide. rising

up a slender timeline
the landscape of possibilities
is becoming visible all around.

## *walls*

are something we have always built.
walls to keep something in
walls to keep someone out

stone axes, arrowheads
faces transformed by hate
masked by friendly glances.

what does history tell us? of walls:
their construction and destruction.
walls – and graves.

which are also a kind of wall
for keeping the dead
on the side they belong.

## bathroom

smash the contours
they designed for you. scrap
the dotted lines, the repetition of form
according to numbers. it looks
like you are free, but still

you keep the silent pointless
arguments inside, try to validate
your opinions, finish your sentences
with a clearly elocuted full stop.

what is right or true
barely interests you at all –
all you want is to
give shape to thoughts

which no one else but you
can, or ever could, form.

*don't let the reins slip*
*from your grip, or lead yourself*
*where you never want to go*

you say in the bathroom
while looking at the mirror
through the mirror – a peephole
which shows an entirely different world.

## bedroom

an early-morning mist surrounds a tranquil house. familiar paths
in the cool mysterious breath. you stand at the window, observe
the yard in surprise – so few shapes you recognise.

in bed the children show their slumbering faces
like they have become someone else for a moment
crossed the borders of their
young lives. how little

you now know of who
they will grow up to be: for a moment
the playground's outlines separate from the mist
then vanish once again from sight.

## attic

all the sketches of everything left unfinished
which occupied your living space (and thoughts)
ever more as years passed by

had to be carried upstairs to the attic
beneath the rafters, amongst sawdust and clothespegs
old spiderwebs, shrivelled-up bat mummies sapped

of life, pigeon shit, cat piss stink
and all the other excessive, unneccessary, unwanted
and forgotten things, so you could finally
move on and feel cleansed.

at night in bed under an eiderdown blanket
you trace the endless repeating pattern
of the rhombuses on the ceiling, you feel the silence
that surrounds your inexplicable feelings of expectation

you sense their power and weight above you
how they impact everything you do next

as you watch their slow unstoppable journey downwards
redrawing and remodeling the rooms of your
sparsely populated consciousness.

## bird cage

you will regret
most bitterly the words left unsaid.
the surface of silence left untouched

by a mouth that opens like a cherry blossom
and ripens into a small sweet fruit.

to ripen, to swallow words like pits
more easily with each passing year

to keep them imprisoned behind vocal cords
like caged birds who never learned
how to sing the right songs –

silence is seemingly golden. you'd like
to open the cage door, whisper to the reeds
all your long-cherished yearnings

but it's already too late:
the cold has taken the blossoms

the wind has ceased giving voice
to your secrets and carrying them
to their rightful place.

## *bridge*

before I reached a safe place
I saw myself falling –

a broken handrail
a crumbling boat dock over a chasm
rusty screws unscrewing themselves
from the rotten planks

I felt the weight
of my body pulling
me down like an anchor

towards the bottom
towards my arrival at the bottom
to a bottomlessness
that might well lie ahead

I felt a hollowness
in the pit of my stomach
like I was descending on a swing or a wave –

the beating of my heart
the dock giving way beneath my feet
the beginning of a journey towards
the future and the unknown.

*stairs*

going down the stairs
I'm always one step ahead of myself.
the conflict between mover and movement

is impossible to solve – why should everything stay the same?
why should anything be renewed through change?

      the choices

that lead to one of these being fulfilled
are like shelves crammed with jam jars –
so similiar and yet so different.

things should stay unchanged here
but still – the potatoes have sprouted white bristling hair

next to the wall a crumpled mouse skeleton
shaped like a crescent moon. something always waxes
something always wanes.

a damp future rises up from the stone floor
past my ankles ever higher, runs over
the top of my rubber boots.

guess which of these it is –
a woman's water breaking
or the beginning of the flood?

## weathervane

becoming ever lighter
I ascend through the smoke
hole, exhale and turn on my back

my wings spread through the atmosphere
like azure fans. down on the ground

a heavenly still summer day –
in a farmer's open palm a small cross-shaped corpse
above a sandstone breast two panes of black eyes

behind the panes
the starry landscapes of deep fields.

inside you tie a silk cord round my beak
hang me from the ceiling so I display
the changes in the weather

but I spin on my axis carelessly like a top –
I don't plan to tell you
anything at all

despite my bird's eye view
of swirling dervish hurricanes and wildfires
wiping old growth forests from land
now dry and burnt. signs

like falling stars
break up into pieces on the threshold

one after the other –
titles, news, articles
books, shows, conferences.

this debate is older than me
but it's up to me to resolve it.

# vivarium

in this landscape I have neither reflection nor shadow. I don't know
where I come from – this house of glass is not my home
more an artificial place or threshold.

an endless sameness in all directions, mute groves of ferns
white branches like torn-off arms – words
no language connects.

in a vivarium a root of thought
feels the shape of the future, discovers
its own strange side. behind a transparent wall

a primate forges a world inside an unforged world
to bring life to a distant lifeless place

but I don't want to leave, I don't need
a new home in cold, dark space.

*solastalgia*

under the roof of August
hangs a tapestry of rye fields – it's there
I stand in the middle of a lean harvest

alien like an outdated map in a place
that's changed. in this new landscape
north's as near as west

black car tyres trundle along unconcerned
spinning round and round

a moment before crashing –
objects in the rear-view mirror
are closer than they appear.

next summer it's not a flood
but a drought. the news says in brief
*this could be the change.* I'm reading a book
where it says it's time to take action –
the future doesn't wait.

on one side of the world someone says
with a look of importance *change
opens up new possibilities.*

on the other side someone cries out –
a voice that's never been heard before.

# ABOUT THE POET

Maarja Pärtna (1986) is an Estonian poet, editor and translator with four poetry collections: *At the Grassroots* (2010), which was shortlisted for the Betti Alver Debut Award, *Thresholds and Pillars* (2013), *[becoming]* (2015) and *Vivarium* (2019). She has won the Juhan Liiv Poetry Award and is the co-founder of the poetry press Elusamus. Her poems, which have been translated into eight languages, weave connections between the human and non-human worlds and address issues of identity and belonging.

# ABOUT THE TRANSLATOR

Jayde Will is a writer and translator from numerous languages. He has an MA in Fenno-Ugric Linguistics from Tartu University, and more than twenty full-length translations to his credit. Recent translations include Latvian poet Artis Ostups's poetry collection *Gestures* (Ugly Duckling Presse, 2018), Lithuanian writer Ričardas Gavelis's novel *Memoirs of a Life Cut Short* (Vagabond Voices, 2018), and Latvian writer Alberts Bels's novel *Insomnia* (Parthian Books, 2020). His own writing can be found at Words Without Borders, In Other Words, satori.lv, Kultūrzīmes, Ubi Sunt, and Lituanus.

# ABOUT THE EMMA PRESS

The Emma Press is an independent publisher dedicated to producing beautiful, thought-provoking books, based in Birmingham, UK. The Emma Press has been shortlisted for the Michael Marks Award for Poetry Pamphlet Publishers in 2014, 2015, 2016 and 2018, winning in 2016.